T0194333

The Song of Beauty

The Song of Beauty

RYAN KENIGSBERG

WESTBOW
PRESS®
A DIVISION OF THOMAS NELSON
& ZONDERVAN

WestBow Press books may be ordered through booksellers or by contacting:

WestBow Press
A Division of Thomas Nelson & Zondervan
1663 Liberty Drive
Bloomington, IN 47403
www.westbowpress.com
1 (866) 928-1240

ISBN: 978-1-9736-6361-4 (sc)
ISBN: 978-1-9736-6348-5 (e)

Library of Congress Control Number: 2019906172

Print information available on the last page.

WestBow Press rev. date: 6/4/2019

INTRODUCTORY COMMENTS:

"'What have I to fear but starvation?' Kino asked.

But Juan Tomas shook his head slowly. 'That we must all fear. But suppose you are correct- suppose your pearl is of great value- do you think then the game is over?'

'What do you mean?'

'I don't know,' said Juan Tomas, 'but I am afraid for you. It is new ground you are walking on, you do not know the way.' "

This quote from Steinbeck's *The Pearl* has a double meaning, both for Kino and his destruction, and for any of those who believe they have found something of great worth. It is a journey. In Steinbeck's story, Kino, a poor fisherman, goes out desperately to the pearl beds because the town doctor will not help his son poisoned by a scorpion. Instead he finds a great pearl and his life changes, ultimately in terrible ways until in mad desperation he at the end of the story flings the pearl back out into the sea.

When I first wrote this story, motivated by Steinbeck's own narrative, I can not say I identified very strongly with Kino's suffering. Now I can see that I do. Are we not those who lose things, often of the utmost importance? Are we not those who are rejected and poor and broken?

This novella references and molds its setting and text after Steinbeck's book, *The Pearl*, which was published by Viking Press in 1947.

I have taken some liberties, following Steinbeck's own pattern. This is a parable, and though everything in it points to an answer, the answers themselves are sometimes revealed by the style of the story itself.

THE SONG OF BEAUTY

"In the city they tell the story of the great pearl –– how it was lost and how it was found again. They tell of Kino, the fisherman, and of his wife, Juana, and of the new baby, Benito. Because the story has been forgotten, it has not taken root in everyone's mind. And, as with all retold tales that are in people's hearts, there are only good and bad things and black and white things and good and evil things and no in-between anywhere.

"If this story is a parable, perhaps everyone takes his own meaning from it and reads his own life into it. In any case, they say that . . ."

CHAPTER 1

Kino awakened in darkness. Night shadowed the land so that even the stars hid. Kino listened, but the night did not answer. All was silent except for the music building in Kino's ears.

The night brought many things with it. Night meant dirty chickens nestled in the hay, pigs sleeping in the muck. Night meant silent birds huddled in the cold, sharks prowling through the pearl beds. Night meant fear, fear stronger than the brush house with its charred twigs and flimsy structure.

Kino closed his eyes. He shook off his weariness and the hauntings of a sleepless night. He touched the bed, as if to remember. He felt for the hanging box where his Coyotito had slept, but turned quickly away. Gone, gone, forever, gone. He turned to his wife so as to forget the word. She was still. He felt her cold hand, perceived her hardened face, touched her disarrayed hair. And he heard the music growing.

Kino's people had once been great makers of songs, songs to tell of the brush houses, the new babies, the great pearls. Some had meanings deeper than life. Eventually his people had stopped making songs, and only remembered them. The songs had meaning and power. Most were good, but others were bad. This morning Kino heard songs that he had never heard before. They were not new, but very old, and very bad. He had never heard them, for they were deeper and older than his time and his people had found ways to forget them.

Kino felt his soul, and it was pounding mightily. The music brought memories so that it cast before him his journey to the sea. He remembered how the scorpion had stung his son. He saw how he had in dreams of saving his family found a great pearl, and how this had promised life for his son and security forever. Then he saw how it had become corrupted.

He saw the evil trackers chasing him, trying to steal from him. He saw his son filling with the poison of the scorpion. And he saw how it had all failed and had left him nothing. His son had died. He had killed a man. He had flung the pearl out, away. He had put his hope in the pearl, and now his soul was gone. He had thrown it away. Now he was a dark shadow of a man who blended with the night. He had left the sea with his face turned aside, its lines formed into a scowl against the mocking of the town. He had wanted to hide, but his house was a pile of ash, and so he had gone to his brother Juan Tomás for help and together they had formed a crooked frame. In it he had hid, but all the night the Song of Evil had grown in his mind. It was very bad.

There was a great rule once taught by the elders of the town, that when one song leaves, another takes its place. So it was that day. The Song of the Pearl had faded and diminished and ceased altogether, a great dream that made a great void. And when Kino heard music again it was the Song of Shame. And when the Song of the Family was gone, in its place was the Song of the Dead Son. And so the Song of Evil was very strong.

Juana was finally arising, her movements almost clumsy. Her eyelashes held weariness as the leaves of the hut held droplets of water, and her face was shadowed with confusion. She rose in a storm and went to where the hanging box would have been. In the darkness was nothing, and the Song of the Family did not fill the void. She paused before the place, and Kino saw it as if she was not awake but dreaming, and fear shook his body. The Song of the Family was gone and in its place was the Song of Fear.

Later when the two had woken enough and the light was enough, they had looked to prepare a breakfast. At first the coal in the fire pit could not be fanned alive. Everything was dead and cold. The cold crept across the floor and Kino could not stop it. He rose, wrapped still in his blanket, with its corners around his shoulders, his head, his face.

As he always did, Kino left the hut to watch the dawn. But today the sun did not rise, for a dark cloud covered the horizon as if there was no sky. Never had Kino seen such cloud. His eyes backed into their sockets, and it was the first time they had moved. He thought of rain and the cracks in the hut, and wrapped the blanket more closely around him.

But for now the sky was mostly clear, and that was enough. Kino sighed. In his ears he heard the waves he had always heard, he saw the fire his wife always built, he felt the blanket he always wore. Some might call him the same man who had always sat there. But then they would not know of those things which are contained in the heart of a man.

Out on the horizon something caught his attention. A ship rising and falling on the waves. A ship with its black mast stark against the darkening background. Kino sat and watched and wondered. He wondered what made the waves rise and fall. What brought the ships here and there. What type of men built such ships, and sailed to such far places. But Kino was a simple man and did not know such answers.

Kino followed Juana in his mind as she prepared, as she always did, the breakfast of corn cakes and pulque. Now she was stooping by the fire and poking aimlessly in the embers. Now she was standing and smiling . . . but today Kino could only see a frown covering her face. He could only see sadness hanging over her movements. This day she was humming the Song of Sorrow. Kino scowled and did not rise. He heard the Song of Evil. And this time it was also the Song of the Broken Family.

Across the brush fence were other brush houses. There other families stirred. There other breakfasts cooked. But those were not where Kino rose and talked and ate. Those huts were not his huts, those pigs were not his pigs, those wives were not his Juana, those children were not . . . But Kino did not have any children.

Few animals were about that morning, for those that could be put in from the storm were in huts, and those that were out were hiding. Even the flock of wild doves had disappeared in the distance. As they flew over, they mocked Kino with their cries and their freedom to fly away from the trouble Kino could not leave. Kino wondered what made storms come and scare birds away, rain and make his son go away, flash and find his soul thrown away. There was no answer. The world was brooding.

Kino arose and went into his brush house. He looked at Juana. Her black hair was carelessly braided and her hands hung limp at her sides, but she was still strong and fierce, ready to fight. Kino squatted by the fire pit and rolled a hot corncake and dipped it in sauce and ate it. And he drank a little pulque and that was breakfast. That was the only breakfast he had ever known outside of feast days, one incredible fiesta of cookies that had nearly killed him, and one lonely breakfast in the woods that had killed his son. He looked again at his wife, and she looked back. But there were no words, for words are insignificant when one can know what the other feels. Then words are empty and pointless. Kino saw in Juana sorrow and fear. And in Kino, Juana saw failure and agony, and that was enough. That was conversation.

After breakfast, Kino went outside again. Juana followed but did not venture past the shadows of the doorway. Kino stretched his back like he always stretched his back and tried to spread himself out to feel the warmth of a new day. But it was still a cold land. The sun cast dim shadows upon the ground, but nothing more. And the pleasant heat which should have been there did not warm Kino this day.

Straining himself, Kino tried to remind himself of a good song. He glanced at Juana, even hopefully, so as to find some song in her. Instantly he turned away, but his eyes could not forget the picture of her darkened face and his ears could not stop the Song of Sorrow from invading his mind.

There he stood, with Juana in the doorway, and the town slowly coming alive. A few houses away there was a bit of laughter, but the hollow air brought it to Kino in a sad and empty way.

Slowly voices arose, detached and hollow. Other voices joined in, and the voices were coming nearer and nearer. Each voice gave a different tone, but all gave the same impression, one which Kino could recognize, the Song of Evil. And it brought fear to the man who had thrown the great pearl away and had not helped the poor town, to the man who had run away and not shared his joy, to the man who had killed another man and fled, to the man who had broken tradition and failed his friends. This man was Kino, and these were his thoughts. These were Kino's own people. Though there were only a score of men now, his mind imagined the group growing and surging and drifting towards him to tell him to go, that they could not live with a murderer, that they would abandon him to the great judges of the town who would pull him down, take him away, and kill him. Were these thoughts true? But it does not matter, for this was Kino and these were his thoughts. He had failed his townsmen, and now he saw them rising up and growing in power like an immense wave coming toward him.

Now Kino was mad. "We must leave," he said, spitting out the words from behind clenched teeth.

Juana had already understood, but she lingered, "We have nowhere to go."

Kino looked with a ferocity out over the town and his people who did not care. He rose up to his full stature, clenched his jaw, puffed his chest and answered in his simple yet profound way, "I am a man." And Juana knew this meant Kino was half-mad, and half-God. She knew that she and Kino would go. She did not question him, for one does not question such a man. Instead she gathered her shawl and joined him. And so two forlorn strangers set out that day, rejected by the town and haunted by many great and terrible troubles.

They skirted the long line of huts, hanging to the shadows. They hurried to leave the cruel place, with the horrible feelings in their stomachs and the heaviness on their hearts, hoping to find peace in separation from humanity. Kino glared menacingly, and felt the blood on his chin from where he was biting his lip.

Soon they did find the shelter of solitude where gazes could not penetrate them. They had turned toward the ocean and presently had left all signs of habitation. And as they approached the ocean, they saw that now the waves crashed down in greater power, for they were the first waves of the great storm. Kino peered far out with his seaman's eye to predict the course of the growing fury and turned away perplexed. Never before had he seen such a storm. Juana drew the shawl tighter around her head as the gusts of wind played with her hair, throwing it rudely around in disordered swirls. She was strong and did not complain. This, she knew, could only be the start of a long and hard journey. A journey harder than the one they had just come from, a journey of trial and pain. A journey with no hope and no promise. A journey where even nature would not receive them.

Often Kino would glance back, afraid the town would discover him, afraid they would demand repayment for the troubles. Afraid they would torment him with their questions. Afraid at how they would angrily demand a share in the wealth he had thrown away and could never recover to appease them. He feared also those cloaked men, the trackers who would hunt him down, requiring his life for the life of the man he had struck down. And so he fled like an animal, and what was behind was more real than what was before him.

They continued along the beach, and their trek was like the beginning of a march through barren land. They stumbled along, and the wind bit at their torn clothes and the sand slashed at them so that they had to guard their eyes. The treachery of the sea flanked them on one side while on the other their fellow man threatened a worse terror. For if a man finds something of great worth and rises above his people, he is respected and revered. His people make songs about him, and come from afar to share in his wealth, his wisdom, and his joy. To watch such a man brings joy enough to satisfy the worn feet of a traveler, to sit and drink with him is to dine with a god. And this was the height to which Kino had attained, where he could have received guests and pitied them with unconcern. He had been the man of the songs, and the songs about the songs, and his wealth promised relief to his people. So they had thought and dreamed. They did not know the great treachery of the pearl. And so when the music of the pearl had faded and when Kino had destroyed its evil, in came the Song of Failure.

Kino wiped away the blood from his lip, but it only kept bleeding. Then he straightened his hunched back and in despairing madness shook his fist at the dark sky, at the storm that could not be stopped, at the blood that stained, at the agony of his heart that bore down upon him. Even so the pain would not stop, and he had to hobble along with increased speed, and the agony of his heart that bore down upon him only grew.

Soon he and Juana came to the canoes tied by the shore. There was his own canoe, the only thing of value he owned in the world. It had been handed down to him from his father's fatherIt meant more than property, for it also meant food and provision. In the past he had thought that with it he could promise Juana security and something to eat. Yet now he knew that this promise was false. It could not save them. The dream did not save poor men like Kino, not even poor men with canoes. He filled with searing rage, and the rage gave him strength, so that he gave his canoe a vicious kick. He turned from it then. What did it matter? For the dream had been sliced to bits by the gaping hole already cut in its bottom.

He remembered with horror the other time he had come down to the sea in his desperation, when he had found the treasure he had been seeking his whole life, the treasure he thought would change his whole life. Kino was silent in this agony, but it rose in him like a fever taking hold. Before him flashed the vision of the pearl, of how it had come to him, how he had fondled it, how his greedy eyes had looked over it and called it precious. But now it was like a nightmare before his eyes, worse, for it was day now, if this could be called day. He demanded peace, but the agony only increased so that he convulsed, his head bobbing up and down, up and down in horror. Now the vision flashed before his mind, how his dirty fist had closed over the pearl and his emotion had broken over him in greedy triumph. To relive it was worse, for now he saw the selfish, corrupted man he had been and the shriveled man he still was. He saw more. How he had put back his head and howled. How his eyes had rolled up and how he had screamed, his body rigid with murderous glee. The sweat of his vision broke out on his forehead as he saw the great evil that was him. His body shook, and he buried his head in his hands. His agony grew until he thought he would die.

Then his wife put her cold hand on his back to steady him, and he slowly relaxed. He remembered the present, and thought hard. Perhaps everything he had known was worse than ever, but he remembered his Juana and her kind touch and relaxed a little more. He looked down at his arms. They still had power. Perhaps there was a way to bring back the good things he had known. But as he started to agree with this melody, he heard the soft sound of the pearl once again, for it was the same. He shuddered again, and no power of money, no strength of might could free him. With another cringe that shook his body Kino looked at his hands. Before him he saw those same hands killing a man, and he looked down with horror upon them as if he was seeing them for the first time. Such fury of dread and despair had never before assailed him. Against him battled a storm so great that the hope of peace was a fleeting thought, an abandoned island in the crashing waves of despair. Had he then thought of it, he would have considered the actual storm hanging over the ocean a minor squall in comparison. He grasped at his stomach as if dying, fell over and rolled around and around in the sand.

Juana could neither offer comfort nor bear to watch his struggle. She closed her eyes against the sight, fell to her knees and wept. Perhaps the two felt more misery than seems reasonable. But when a couple has lost their child, when they have lost their friends, then the burden they bear is almost too great for comfort. They are forlorn, alone, removed. When, however, this loss is everything they have, when they have lost the last melody of hope, when their dream has faded and extinguished, then their despair is too great to be imagined. Then they are dead, and yet they must go on living. Even the kindest of hands cannot touch a sore so deep and horrible without the touch causing intense pain.

And horrors bring with them again other horrors. The power of the dream had engulfed Kino and so when it had torn, so had he. His soul was contained in the pearl, so that removing the pearl made it as though he were dead. The dead man who lives thinks he has lost everything, but then he realizes he must suffer existence. Abandoned by all else, Kino's agony only cloaked him all the more.

Faint voices sounded far off in Kino's mind. They were real voices, from the world he once knew and even loved. Not just the voices of his past, but now of men who had come from the town after him. In the storm the voices twisted and carried, twisting with malevolent bitterness, cutting

the tormenting wounds of Kino again and again. Kino forgot for a moment his despair, for he heard again the Song of Evil approaching. An observer might think that evil could not hurt the poor man anymore, but then he would have been absolutely contained in the Song of Evil. Kino could still hear the song, and this meant that more could come, indeed that more was on its way. Though wherever he went, the Song of Evil would follow him and be in him, he would still run from its power. Though the shadow was in him, he was not yet shadow.

He rose and looked at Juana, "they have come." The trackers. Those men who had tormented Kino, who had hunted him in the night of his son's greatest peril. Their voices filled the air with dread. Each syllable caught in the wind and shrieked, and the evil coming was greater than the evil that had already arrived. Kino heard the word called after him, "murderer." In agony he looked at his hands, as if the torment of their voices chanted "look at yourself, guilty, guilty, guilty." He saw on his hands the blood from his bleeding lip. His eyes peeled wide and he tried to back away from his hands as if the evil was foreign to him. But now the blood on his hands called out to him, "murderer," so that he could not escape. The Song of Evil had touched him, had hurt him, and now he saw that he had even accepted its touch and was becoming a part of it. Now he rose as in a dream, and the emotion broke over him. He put back his head and howled. His eyes rolled up and he screamed and his body was rigid.

Then he fled. He fled from the Song of Evil, but everywhere he went, the song came with him. Now its fingers grabbed out at him, and it rose up from inside him. Nowhere was refuge offered, and the men came after him. Even his wife was gone now, though who can say from which storm she had fled, that of seeing her broken Kino or of the breaking gale. Kino looked up, and saw that the sun had made itself scarcely visible through the clouds. It is not useless to describe further the great horror that this man of a tribe felt when even the sun hid from him, if we understand his agony and bear his misery. The man was like a wild man, running from destruction before and behind. Here was a man, and though his life hung in the balance, nobody cared. In the town they scorn a mad man, and distance themselves from him. In the town Kino was worse than a madman, for he was a madman and cruel. Kino lived a horror worse than any nightmare, for the terror was constantly before him, in mind and body and spirit. The blackness of hate bent down upon him and it rose within him as he shook his fist, but this time it gave him no strength, so into the sand he staggered and fell. The Song of Evil was very strong, and the trackers swarmed toward him and the great storm circled toward him and the trackers and the storm were in a race to devour him.

Now the great storm came bringing a fury which none could withstand. Wave after wave broke upon Kino, huddled alone on the beach. Kino felt its power and felt the fear it brought and wondered what could bring such power, what could match such fear. And the pattern of the waves became a great collapsing and crashing as the water erupted in huge billows of foam and then came down again in hard pellets that formed dents in the sand. Torrents of rain came and beat upon Kino's back and face and arms. So great was the storm that the trackers fled before it in fits of horror, leaving Kino alone and helpless. It was as if the storm spoke and said, "Who can stand before me; who can last my fury?" "Not I, not I," Kino wept, "no one can." But then he wondered what could cause the storm and send the seas racing, what force could master the sea and tell it where to go. The rain formed rivers, and these rushed down the sand toward the sea, and here the waves would meet them, as if trying to push the water back upon the land. Wave after wave broke upon Kino, and he fought to keep the power from engulfing him in its might. His whole body was overcome in the power and fury of the waves, and he knew that he could neither match the power before him nor stand and answer the sea's challenge.

One moment he would try to escape the fury and run up the embankment, but then the waves would catch him and pull him back again. And the arms it grabbed Kino with were too great to be resisted, so that he sunk down in the sand and whirled backwards. Then he would submit, thinking that perhaps here was his chance to escape, as if death could be his refuge. Then he would let the waves draw him out, but as he neared death he would see its ugly face and see that this was no relief. Again he would struggle. His confused mind would argue this way and that, as irregularly as the swirling of the seas breaking upon a great rock. Here before him was a force which drove upon his body with such magnitude that it left his mind detached from the troubles of his own life. As the world groaned Kino's little miseries were lost within its power as little Kino was lost within the giant breakers. The storm spoke to him, "How dare you to pity yourself!" In the presence of its voice the troubles of the past slowly faded, drowned out by the bellowing power. Before Kino had thought the storm would bring relief to his struggles, but now he saw that the fury inside of it was worse than the fury of his foes. He saw that the power driving the seas was more awful than his own power so that it could snap him in a moment and send him away.

Before the storm his previous agony now grew more awful, rising to the heights of the breakers and the dimensions of the boundless ocean. Kino would fall and crumble before the enormous breaths of the sea as it swept him off his feet and plunged him under the water, and then the sea would breathe out allowing Kino to struggle to his feet for the next tumbling wave. And the breathing was filled with voices, "You deserve this. You have earned this." And Kino could only weep in agreement. He would try to forget this, and instead consider the good things he had known in the town–the people, the family, the church, the animals, maybe even one or two of the foreigners. Maybe he could even make himself grateful for the doctor. For a town is something secure, something safe, and Kino needed something to hold him safe.

Kino looked out and saw how the ship tossed upon the water. His thoughts wandered to the canoes on the beach, how they weathered the storms with ease. Ropes held them down, held them in place so they could weather any storm. Kino decided a town was like a rope, for it held its people together. A town gave meaning and unity, as if holding the people to itself. Indeed, everything good he had known was like a rope that held one together, the doctor, the town, the family, and even life itself. Then the futility of his thoughts shone before him and screamed at him, "This is not enough." He knew his error. He remembered how the doctor had hurt his Coyotito, what kind of rope was that? He remembered how his town had so easily sliced him from the rope, and he did not want to return again to that sort of rope, a rope that would abandon. That is not a stabilizing rope, only a sort of false thread, an animal promising security and then deserting you when you have given away everything to it for its pledge. His family had not been a rope strong enough to hold together; his family had collapsed. Even the rope of life, which the elders of his town had spoken of, had released him; it had abandoned him to the sea. No, there could not be a rope. There was no Song of the Rope. What rope does anything but bind?

This was how the man Kino thought, and just as he had hoped in something to stabilize him, his thoughts plummeted again before him. He looked out, and at last the cloud swallowed the ship into its foreboding murkiness. Then another wave, greater than the rest, rose before him, and it towered up and up and up, and to Kino who had never known anything like it, to Kino who saw before him a hopeless tunnel of destruction, to Kino who had lost town, and church, and friend, to this man Kino the wave rose and made him tremble, and then as it towered to that great height it paused for a second as if considering, and then it made up its mind and collapsed, coming down upon him as if to settle the last and final blow.

CHAPTER 2

All storms pass, for that is the way of the earth. All waves rise, and then they fall. All struggles climax, and then they fall. But there are certain things that do not pass. Some storms last forever. Some things that are broken can never be fixed. Some people fall asleep and do not wake up. Though all storms pass, to the town and the families and the people the storms last longer. When storms bring death and destruction, when storms bring hurt and loss, the towns and the families and the people must live in the results of the storm. Sometimes this is as bad as the storm, for the storm passes on, but the house is gone, the son is lost, and the people must live in a changed and newly broken world.

Kino lay in the sand on the beach, and the waves lapped slowly over his feet and legs, his torso, his arms, and his face, its mouth gaping open. His left leg stuck out at an odd angle, his arm bent under his body, and his neck curved down, pressing his face in the sand. The tide came in and gently picked Kino up and lay him down again. Powerful waves had been replaced by the smooth lapping of the ocean. It rose peacefully and then sighed with calm breaths, the gentle yawns after a nightmare. The waves lifted him and settled him down again as if breathing for him. Each wave did a little to untwist his leg, to free his arm, to straighten his neck. The sea lapped over his face and wiped away the blood; a kind hand had finally come and with care renewed his torn body. It took away the dirt, and someone was wiping a clean cloth over him. It removed the sweat, and it was a kind mother pouring cool water over her tired boy. But the sea was not a mother, and the sun that warmed Kino's body was not a mother. They were only gifts.

Kino opened his eyes softly and saw the bright sun so that he shut them again. The sun felt good. Again he opened his eyes, and this time a small cloud shaded the light. A cloud–it reminded him of the agony. But somehow the warmth of the sun and the softness of the cloud made it easier to forget such things than remember them. Somehow the new day made these tragedies seem small and unimportant.

He held up his hand–the blood was gone. He felt his lip. Even the swelling had left. Then he relaxed a little. He could not hear any of the ancient songs, but he could feel the soft sand, and the warm sun, and the soothing waves. And his body relaxed, even though his mind was still wary. In his mind he struggled, and did not find such relief. A sudden pang of emotion struck over him and he rose to his feet and looked around, as if looking desperately for something he had lost. He stood there, his half naked body covered in torn clothes, his hands dangling limp at his side, his feet still in the water that played with them and created patterns in the sand, sucking away at his feet. He was a ghost, a wandering ghost without hope or home but only ceaseless torment. And he looked like a haggard old man deeply burdened, like a crippled old man finding no one to hold him up and no child to bring him joy.

But the day was clear and pleasant, and to the ghost on the beach the sun played kindly enough. Clouds threw their shadows upon the sand in long waving spirals. And then the sun would break out again and the water would reflect a great brilliance of sparkling diamonds. These points of light hurt Kino's eyes, and he would put his hand to his face to shade his eyes. After the long darkness the brightness hit him with little stunning shocks. But it was so beautiful he could not shut his eyes. Something caught Kino's attention, something bobbing on the water. He thought maybe it was a canoe, and thought perhaps its cord had broken in the storm. So he swam out towards it, and his ghostlike body glided through the water, up and down, for he had swum many times and practiced to make his swimming smooth. In fact it was a canoe. He got in and rested in the shade under the lip of one side, and the canoe was to him a mattress reminding him of a bed and a home where he could live secure. And beneath him was the great mattress of the world, the ocean, and on it he rocked lazily.

Sharks swam in the waters, and their fins he could just make out in the distance, and he considered the dolphins and how they fought the sharks, and he thought of the men of the town who fought the sea, and for their efforts brought home food for their families. To Kino who had always been a fisherman, this work had seemed good, but now he saw it as an endless struggle. He was still young. But already he bore the marks of a man scarred by time. Muscles still lined his body. But bruises spoiled their strength. They were the signs of toil; not of victory, but of endless, haunting struggle like the struggle of an animal caught in a barbed fence. After the ocean generously offered its wealth it would come back to kill and destroy.

Before long the sun gained strength and beat down upon the man lying in the canoe so that he grew warm and water droplets formed upon his forehead. Finally, he groped out of his laziness, like a restless man who can not forget the nightmares of the past, and considers how refreshing it would be to feel the cool water over his back again. Such a man as who wants to feel freshness and relief, and forget the trials and the hurt. And so the man dove into the sea. Some moments like these, when the sea is calm and lazy and we are unaware, great things are at work.

CHAPTER 3

So Kino closed his eyes and slipped into the water, and the coolness rushed about him and woke him from his thoughts. As the sun had warmed his back and then began to lower in the sky, the current had carried Kino toward the pearl beds so that now as he swam underwater and reached out his hands, he expected to feel the clams he had always felt. His fingers closed around something hard, a long plank, jutting out from the ocean, and the surprise of finding it brought fear throughout his stiffened body. He felt how cold was the water, and its unfamiliarity made him shudder, wondering what might lurk in the shadows. He had but time to feel briefly the rough surface before resurfacing to gasp for breath.

As he looked down, he forced his eyes open and saw many more planks, and he remembered the ship that had only days before sailed elegantly on the waters. The storm had taken that image of splendor and smashed it like a flimsy toy. Now the hull marked the pearl beds as a gloomy grave, and the country, and the families, and the friends of the sailors would look out in some distant land and wonder what became of the ship that never returned and of the sailors who would never wave again.

Kino gasped then, for he had seen in the pearl pictures of greatness such as these so as to make him envy the foreigners. And yet now they too faced loss. But then what built great ships, and what guided great men? To Kino, this wonder was the greater of the two. He imagined the great people far away and could not understand how they too could experience grief, how they too were defeated by the waves.

Here the Song of Evil was strong, and its dread surged over Kino. In his mind Kino imagined himself the master of a great ship. But the ship was corrupt. And in the dream Kino clenched something, and he would not let go or show it to the light. He considered it as of great value, as a deliverer to his family, and did not care for the destruction of others.

But these thoughts grew and twisted until the thing he clutched became some great evil and when he looked at the thing it was a pearl in his hand, a great gnarled pearl, and it ruled over his mind, and it beat the rhythm of his heart, and it commanded the actions of his feet. Then he knew why it seemed a great dream the sailors lived, how it looked wise but was folly and how it could crumble so swiftly.

Dreams are powerful things and do not leave so easily or fall so quickly as power or might. For the great pearl in the vision did not leave Kino. It held onto him even though it beat the Song of Evil. And since the black pearl also was the heart that beat the rhythm of Kino's body, the Song of Evil beat in Kino and welled up and left him weak and corrupted and twisted. But this, though it left Kino weaker and smaller, this power grew and grew and would not leave Kino. Now Kino thrashed in the water with a clouded mind, and his heart beat slower, and his feet became weak. The pearl promised good things to Kino, but every time he thought he would see some good thing, the dream would fade, like a mirage which at last twists into disappointing reality. There were stories of these mirages in the village, how something beautiful would glow and then twist and disappear. Kino would see his son again, and when he would open his arms to embrace his son, the son would disappear and a black scorpion would be in his place, and it would sting Kino with a pain more venomous than any poison of this world.

Kino's thoughts were not entirely black. He knew that if there was something still to be lost, then there was something still that was had. Kino looked and looked for the good to be found, but he saw only blackness around him. Some moments like these, when the heart is hurt and broken, and the darkness does not fade, and the mind least expects it, in times like these great things are at work. These moments are rare, but when the sun breaks through and shines down upon a hurting man, then the light is more brilliant for the darkness, for then it blinds the eye with its glory. Here was a man who had fallen and was left broken and torn, so that the dreams he had known had faded and the sun he knew had darkened and the sea he had worked in had risen up against him. Here was a man who did not know hope. Sometimes in these times, when we are dark, when we have fallen off the cliff of goodness and are left abandoned by everything in the world, then great things outside of the world are at work.

This day the sun shone down. It slit away the clouds and opened a small gap in the clouds, and it shown upon a patch of the sea, and that patch was on a certain canoe, Kino's canoe, and below him was a graveyard, but whoever sent the sun was greater than the graveyard.

Kino felt the sun and looked up, and he wondered what the sun meant in shining here. He did not know that good sometimes comes to change the darkness, even if it is often not the good hoped for or expected. The ray flashed upon the surface of the sea and bent in the water, and it shown upon the sand at the bottom of the ocean. And Kino stood and wondered as the rays of the sun bounced and frolicked, and the sun danced upon Kino, and the light and the shadow made beautiful shapes and patterns, and it made Kino look beautiful, and the water bent and corrected his body so that it looked like he too danced. Kino held out his hand, and now the blood was gone and in its place light frolicked, not that this light was so great in itself, but that it carried a joy greater than broken men and huge waves and even light itself, as if the light held the great power of the sun and the mystery of its power, as if it was part of the sun and yet only a small part, and still the light reflected the sun with great brilliance. And as the light had come a long way and kept descending in full and continuous joy from the sun, so Kino's soul began to wonder up and up to great things.

Kino saw the light that had come to him, and he watched it play games in the sand, and he saw that where the light flickered on the seabed there was something he had not seen there before, a part of the wreck. It danced there in the water, for it was in the patch of light as well. Kino dove down, and he held his breath and felt the exhilaration as the water pushed upon him. He reached the object and tugged upon it, and he felt its hard smooth edges and the coldness of its surface, and he tried to unbury it. It was heavy, and full with sand, and he had to dive again and again before he made any progress. But the object rewarded his efforts and slid out from its place in the ocean. Indeed, some treasures are hidden like this, deep in the depths of the oceans, covered and forgotten, left alone and forsaken. These treasures are abandoned while men chase other treasures.

What had Kino found? It rested softly upon the sand, and Kino dove again to examine it. It was a chest, not a great big chest or a grand decorated chest, nor a chest to carry gold and silver. In fact it was rather a small box. And Kino wondered what it could contain, and if he dare to open it. For he remembered the pearl he had found which had looked good but had turned black, and he wondered if any light could shine in his life again, or if a new wonder could provide any true hope, and shed light like a lamp upon his heart. He wondered if the dreams contained in this box were any better than the dreams he had known that had crumbled. Yet as he looked at the humble furnishings, and the careworn handle, and the carefully carved wood, Kino did not sense the lurking power of harm. It was as if its simplicity and gentle beauty could only contain good. Indeed, the simple box would have at first seemed useless and insignificant, or so Kino would have thought had his mind still been filled with the empty promises of the black pearl. He considered. Something about the chest's gentleness and softness, its unassuming exterior and meekness–these did not sound like the Song of Evil.

Then Kino heard it. It was a new melody: the Song of Beauty.

Those who have never heard this song might not recognize its incredible loveliness. For this song is one of the most ancient songs, and its richness is greater than any other song, but the town had long forgotten it and had rarely known its wonder. The Song of Beauty is not the song of apparently beautiful things, like pearls and woman. It is not the song of false beauty, like the doctor and the scorpion. It is not the song of temporary beauty, like families and friendships. For this song is much deeper, and in it is a melody of joy and hope and life. When the song comes to a pearl or a woman, or a great many other things, it makes them truly beautiful. It makes a pearl a reminder of something more beautiful, and it makes a woman's heart a picture of purity. Such a song should be remembered every day, and yet the people of the town had forgotten it. For it is gentle and graceful so that if one chooses one may easily forget it. The Song of Beauty is different than all other songs, for other songs come when unwanted, but the Song of Beauty comes only gently and humbly.

The people of the town forgot the song for a more dangerous reason. The Song of Evil wars against the Song of Beauty, so that only one song can be heard at a time. Though at first those who hear the Song of Beauty love it with fondness, it takes time to grow in the heart and increase in magnificence. Often the people of the town say they love the song, but then greed or some other darkness enters them and the Song of Beauty grows faint in their ears, and sometimes forgotten entirely. The Song of Beauty is great, but the Song of Evil always seeks to destroy it.

When Kino first looked upon the pearl and greed grew in his heart, the Song of Beauty could not give music to his ears. When he had dreamed of the pearl's power, he had forsaken this song. As Kino thought of these things, he wondered whether this new treasure was the same, if there was any hope or just a longer deception. And then he decided to open the box, the box from the ship from across the sea, from the place where they built great ships. Kino opened the chest. And here a different journey begins, a new journey, a journey as deep as the ocean bed and as strong as the ocean current, for we have as yet only described a little what is the Song of Beauty.

Kino brought the chest to the surface. He sat there staring at it in his canoe, and then he opened it. He felt the smooth inside of the chest and saw how its sides were carefully covered with a soft fur covering and imagined the careful touches of the man who must have held a deep reverence for the chest. Resting in the soft material was a humble book, its cover made of leather, its edges worn, its pages damp. Engraved on its lower right corner were two words which Kino could barely make out. Perhaps the reader already knows them. It says, The Pearl. Kino gently shut the lid, for he had decided to pack the chest away and take it with him. Immediately the Song of Beauty faded, and immediately the Song of Evil came as a great challenge, trying to drown out the music. It tempted Kino to think that he had never owned a book before, so that he drew it selfishly to himself, and he sat there stunned by the power of the evil so that he was lost in its power.

Again the sun beamed down on him, and he remembered to forget himself and his little dreams so that he opened up his mind to better things. Then he did not want to hide the chest away, but to look again at the book and read its pages. He drew the chest closer and again opened it, so that the Song of Beauty began to grow in his mind. His eyes were opened to the idea of hope and of glory, and he remembered how beautifully the sun shone. When he looked at the book, the Song of Beauty welled up and grew and rose, and though it seemed so humble and even insignificant, this was the way the song rose, and Kino looked up and in his native tongue said, "Yes." He looked at the ocean, and thought how marvelous were the waves, and he looked at the sand on the shore and wondered how he could have ever failed to see such marvelous intricacy. Kino even looked down at his hands, and when he saw them he marveled even more, for not only did he not see blood and guilt on his hands, but this time as he looked at them he stared with awe to see their wonderful design and ability.

Kino thought of what the book contained, and he gasped and wondered with joy at its contents. He wondered at what The Pearl was worth, not its worth to sell, but a much deeper worth that he would never sell, and yet could share with others, and Kino knew The Pearl was far greater than any pearl he had found before.

Again, the book's melody rose inside of Kino, and he began to understand what love meant. Kino's hands opened wide, and his heart opened wide, and he held the book up and was silent so that the music fell upon a receptive heart. The power of the music contained within him was a calm force but strong enough to break mountains and stop seas. There he floated, and the mystery he had sought and failed to find, and the mystery he had forgotten and forsaken, and the mystery he had buried in the sea became real to him. What could this book contain, but the joy which was already so freely given to Kino. Kino knew he was changed, and he sat motionless, jaw hanging, eyes locked, soul racing.

He thought that had the sailor known how great was this book, he would have never even put it in a chest, but held it close to him every day, and shared its contents with others, and even brought it across the sea to Kino. And though the sailor must have been a wonderful man, Kino knew that something greater must have brought this treasure, and he smiled to think of it.

Here a story has ended, for the darkness of Kino's soul and the darkness of his heart had been confronted with the great light, the pearl greater than the world. The story of Kino's past had come to a conclusion. But when one story ends, another begins. When the story of the worthless pearl had run its course and destroyed Kino and brought him low and even close to death, then another pearl found him. This pearl was another sort of pearl, and in its power were things inexpressible and grand. Its truth covered Kino so that he forgot his past, and it brought him into the light of day. This was life, this was stability, this was a better journey, and the Song of Beauty grew in Kino's soul and it gave him dreams to see beauty in everything. But in all this we have hardly said anything and have not even left the world of dreams.

Besides, though Kino did not think of it, he should have remembered that in the shadows around him the Song of Evil lurked and waited for a chance to snatch away his joy.

CHAPTER 4

All journeys have a reason and a force behind the journeying. Before Kino had attempted to use his own power to journey on, and his journey had taken him to the face of death. Now as Kino considered his situation, he realized how bleak and painful it was, how he would have to explain himself and repay, and as he thought of these things fear and anxiety welled up within him. Fear and anxiety do not accomplish anything but to make one afraid and anxious. Here we must oblige the reader to read what the writer can only tell. It is more readily learned by experience and is harder to show, and some must be told with parable. Here we make many mistakes, for it is hard to define with words what can only be known. Perhaps the reader will accept this rude apology. We do not know, but this time Kino tried to face his fears and tried to rest, and as he began to delight in the Song of Beauty he found more peace. He knew that this new power was more powerful than anything he had known, and so he went, trusting. Something pushed him on and said that this was worth it.

As the sun lowered in the sky and peace calmed the ocean and made its surface smooth, Kino saw men coming down towards the water. He could have hid, he could have run away, but at this point Kino knew that the only way to overcome fear was to face it. Kino paddled toward the shore, and he kneeled in the sand as the trackers approached him, and he waited for their threats. The trackers came and yelled at him, and asked him why he did not run, and when he replied, "I can not keep running," they became angry and came down and grabbed him and took him away.

They carried him up past the canoes and the beach and the grass and carried him towards the town, back to the world Kino had fled from. When a man flees a place, it is not a good thing to be brought back, for it means that the man is a prisoner of a place he would prefer to have never seen again. Each step hurt Kino in this way, but somehow he knew that this way, the hard way, was the best, and he found comfort in the Song of Beauty and what it had done for him, and more importantly what it was doing for him. What did the Song of Beauty do in such a place, when to some it seemed that the song had abandoned him? These things are great mysteries and require great explanations, but to Kino who did not know of great things or how the world worked or why evil men held him in his hands, the Song of Beauty meant comfort, raw, heart- enveloping comfort when dragged through the worst streets. The Song of Beauty meant security, because though externally things fell apart, Kino could remain held in the beauty of the music. And the Song meant presence, that it would never leave or abandon Kino but instead go with him in the hardest spot and the worst place and even still hold him up.

The news came to the town. It spread from mouth to mouth, and the people who heard flocked out hungrily to satisfy their curiosity. Some had harbored bitterness, and so flung stinging words at Kino. Some mocked him, saying, "Where is your pearl now?" He was dragged and mocked before them as one going to his death, and the rocks and stones tore at him as the procession moved along the hard dirt road.

Instead of hearing their insults, Kino smiled for the first time thinking of the beauty he had in the awful moment. And so, in the midst of the danger and the treachery, the bitter words and the glaring looks, when the world around Kino had fallen on top of him and had called him thief and failure and abandoner and fool and weakling, then he was able to hear for the first time how fragrant was the sound of the Pearl, and he was able to hear the words, "You are loved; you are secure; you are mine." Kino delighted in the music and it was a new wonder to him greater than anything he had known and more powerful than the best things he had ever dreamed. As he delighted, the dream rose and unfurled within him so that he smiled. Now he looked at the people, not afraid of their glances or their mocking words. Now he cared for them. The transition was gradual, for Kino had never known such feelings before. His smile was crooked, and his love twisted. His ears hardly noted even the simplest notes of the music. In Kino a new song had started, and a start does not need to be magnificent.

The progression of citizens continued along the streets, and Juana was among them. Tears streaked her face, for she had wept all night. When she joined the progression, it was not to scorn or to mock or to blame, but to weep with Kino and feel his hurt, for her love moved beyond selfishness so that she glowed to see Kino happy and wept to see him cry. Juana did not want Kino to see her, for after some trials, reunion can be hard. And so she skirted the crowds, sad and depressed. She had tried to offer everything she had for Kino, and at first she thought she had done well. She had cooked his meals and brought a child to his world, and she had rejoiced in his victories. Then hardship had come, and though Juana could face hardship, she could not prevent it. And though she could care for her husband when he fell she could not pick him up. For a wife who has loved so deeply, the pain is felt just as deeply. Though it is hard, to love deeply is worth it.

When Juana looked at Kino, she saw a man mistreated, slung between the arms of angry men who hated him. His arms would pull out at painful angles, and his feet would drag behind so that his knees and feet would bump on the ground. His head bent down under the pain and the dust covered his legs and his hands and his face. Then he smiled, and when he smiled Juana froze in shock and wonder. She could not even remember the last time she had seen him smile, and yet here in the dirt and the grime he smiled, and she wondered what could change a man so. Eagerly she plunged through the crowd to get close r to this man, and as she came to the front of the group, his head was slung so that his face looked upon her and their gaze met. Kino smiled again with joy to see his wife, and Juana also started to smile but then she frowned. This joy she could not understand nor accept, this joy that was so easy.

That day a man had begun a journey, and no force could stop him. The priest came out to Kino and reprimanded him for his greed and his lack of faith. Kino heard the words and immediately forgot them, letting the fruitless words fall on the street. Instead he looked back at the priest and smiled and thanked him for the duties he fulfilled. The priest fell back astonished at what he had seen, for this was something new, something he had never heard.

Here in the dirty streets marched an important progression, unaware that they bore not a destroyed man but a renewed man. When the doctor came out on his balcony and curled his fat lip in a dirty way and scorned Kino, the criminal responded with grateful words, thanking the doctor for his good work and even inquiring how the doctor had been doing. Those in the crowd did not see these things or notice these things, and if they had they would not have understood them. Then they could have seen that the broken people were those like the priest who spoke of God but did not know him, like the doctor who sought riches but did not see the people before his very own eyes, did not see the poor and humble people he could have helped. These men were the criminals and the chained, who had looked to all the wrong places.

They had come to Kino once when they thought he could offer them riches. What they did not understand was that then Kino had nothing. Now in his hand was a gift more beautiful than what they had sought before, but they thought him a scoundrel. Indeed he had once been a scoundrel, and had done things not worth mentioning and brought calamity to himself, but when the calamity caught up to him and punished him for the crime, it found a new man. He deserved the punishment and wrath for his crime, and so Kino gladly awaited the punishment, knowing the need for justice. But he also understood the secret that this system of justice only punished him temporarily, and that he would one day live in the Song of Beauty untouchable from any law.

Here is a tale of contrasts where a man experiences life for the first time as he is led off to the dark road to prison. It is not a rare story, though one that is not told often. Was Kino really free? This is a mystery too great to explain in common words, and few will use or listen to uncommon words, but time will reveal the true nature of his story. That day one man in a crowd was led to the prison, where the storm clouds had gathered and threatened to destroy and punish, and the great chiefs sat and debated whether this man should die or this one should not. But some storms end, and some storms leave flowers. They threw him in the prison and left him at last, for the crowd had tired of jeering. The townspeople did not hear Kino's words, for they were busy and distracted and had forgotten. But perhaps a few noticed, perhaps a few heard. "I believe," Kino said.

CHAPTER 5

everal nights later a phantom skirted the prison and approached Kino. It was Juana. She sat in the dirt beside him, separated by the long iron bars stretching up from the ground. Together they sat, and the silence was not enough on its own to bind them together, for understanding is not strong enough to hold a family together, and mutual love is not strong enough to hold a marriage together. That cord had broken. For what does it mean to understand when hurt comes, what is it worth to love when the world is crumbling? Now it was not that they chose silence, but that they did not know anymore how to talk. Juana felt alone. In the darkness they could not see each other and there was an emptiness about it. Juana knew that the man who had stood strong before could never stand strong enough to hold her together. For this she wept. Upon her mind flashed again the vision of Kino when he had been brawny and wild, free to provide for the family, free to protect her. His strength then had not been enough, she knew, and decided she would not hold on to the dream of the past. When the world of their lives had been destroyed, burned to the floor, they sat together, and they could not find words to describe it. But Juana felt more like she was alone than together, more separated than connected. She had always tried so hard, and now after all her effort all she had won was misery.

Then Kino held her hand, but it was not how he had held her in the past, when he had been half god and half mad and his touch had been that of a fierce bull. Now he held her gently, and his gentleness was somehow stronger than his past strength. His gentleness dug down deep into her heart, and it picked her up. Then Kino forgot the emptiness and smiled at Juana, and though Juana could not see him smiling in the dark, she could feel it shining there. It shocked her so that she jumped back a little, but then at length its kindness grew on her and she smiled back. And when Juana smiled in this land of darkness, new life rose in her, and she sat in awe at what her Kino was becoming. She sat in awe at the joy that was inside her, and she could not explain it.

Juana had always been strong, with great will-power. Her strength had never been in joy, but in a spirit hardened against the surrounding chaos and failure. Her mind wandered to these things, and to the strength within her, and suddenly pride began to creep into her heart. She focused on her ability, and it filled her with glee to think of her determination. Kino noted a change. He sensed how quickly her joy was slipping away, and the man in him roared against the approaching evil that threatened to again steal Juana's joy. As he raged the Song of Evil rose up in his heart as well, for he had forgotten that the only way to defeat the Song of Evil was to hear the sound of another song, the stronger song, and to do this he would need to relax in another's strength, in another's song. So he sat still and tried to listen, and at length he heard the melody again. He gently squeezed Juana's hand. He showed her something other than pride, and though Kino could not see the change, he knew she felt something better than pride. As this new sense grew in her heart, of hope and appreciation for something better, she heard the melody as well, and when at length she thought about the change she noted with surprise how quickly the pride had fled.

Then Kino opened her hand and placed in it the book that had found him, and she received, at last knowing that here was a rope stronger than any Kino could provide, and that only as Kino humbled himself and trusted in this rope, that only then would he have strength. She wondered if maybe this was the strength that held him up, that had carried him along the road of terrors and grasped his hand when he had haltered, and that this power was a power stronger than all that Juana had known. She clutched the book tightly and wondrously, and then the phantom was gone.

Juana left Kino and was enveloped in the darkness of the night. She left gently, full of a soft cheerfulness and quietness. Her arched back had lost its defiance, her shoulders had lost their straightness. Now she was strong without being strong, for the strength was not from her but rather through her, as if now she did not have to stand with her back rigid against the crashing of waves, the waves of fear, failure, and despair. Instead another sort of wave was picking her up so that though she relaxed she traveled farther. These were the waves of joy in hardship, strength in weakness, beauty in brokenness, victory in defeat. Though all had crashed upon her she walked as one restored.

Kino also saw this transformation and marveled. Before he had only felt a great surge within himself, but now he saw the great surge pouring out of him to touch others. Before he had only felt restored, but now he saw redemption, and to him the restoration in his wife was a joy too great to fully explain. This joy rose and grew and soared within his soul so that he could have said that his heart had become so full that it would burst. But still it filled larger and larger, and the ecstasy he felt was a wonder that few can explain, for few have swam in those deep waters and rushing waves where love impacts hardship, transforms weakness, cleanses brokenness, and covers defeat. Here, where darkness abounded and covered the face of the earth, another idea had taken hold and it was a marvel for him to behold. Suddenly the past which had brought despair had been replaced by life which birthed newness and hope. Never again would anything destroy Kino's family, not because of his great nobility or courage, but because his family had been rescued by a beauty far beyond any power to destroy. Now it was only a matter of getting closer to that star. And when both Kino and Juana embraced the same star, the Song of Beauty, then they became closer themselves. Though they might be isolated stars in the skies of that simple nation, suddenly the darkness separating their pinpoints of light were eclipsed in the brilliance of a sun that held them together with blinding beauty. Here a family could grow, and thrive, and could repair the frustration.

To Kino who sat in prison in awe of this transformation, to Kino who had been an outcast and a failure, to this simple man Kino came this dream, and the Song of the Family flared in his ears. This time, however, was different, for the music that came to him came from a higher source and a higher power. He had given up and in giving up on his weakness he had found another strength that would hold his family together. For the Song of the Family had become a part of hearing the Song of Beauty.

For the first time Kino was a man, and Juana was a woman. Not that they had not been before, but that they had been corrupted. Only a few have seen this type of change, or perhaps it is more true that only a few have appreciated this newness. Indeed, perhaps it is not that they have failed to appreciate it, but that they have not understood it. There are many pearls in this world, for there are many valued treasures. The people of the town chased after these treasures for they sparkled and danced and were good. But they were not perfect. So the families had crumbled. Fathers left their families when they saw a pearl to chase, mothers forsook their motherhood when they saw a treasure to have. They had done this not because they did not love their family, nor because they did not value their role, but because in the shortness of life they had found other pearls that they preferred. Not that these other treasures were bad, but that they were not perfect.

Kino understood this as well, and for the first time he became one of those wise men who see differently and explain to us who do not know. He whispered a few words, and the words were very powerful. They were not grand or magnificent; instead they were simple. They were not confusing philosophy; indeed a child could understand them. Rather he sighed, breathing in with a sort of gasp at what he had realized, and then he breathed out again in a voice hardly audible, "the pearl that holds every other pearl together." It was a whisper, a whisper that we could easily miss, that could have been said again and again in our hearing and that we would have never recognized. It was the answer to a mystery, a mystery we have never solved and yet is always answered if we were to listen. But we forget to listen. There under the stars that represented the haphazard confusion of life, a man saw that what had found him was a star that held all other stars in place and made every other star sparkle in complete order and glory. Only some have fathomed this mystery, only a few have heard this whisper.

Kino was still alone in the darkness, and little did he know of what lay out under the arches and hidden behind houses. Shadows moved over the ground, and the shadows were men. The Song of Evil is strong during the night. It sneaks into doorways and crouches behind sleepers. It draws men out to do vile deeds, and it draws a blanket over people's minds.

That night the doctor hurried out on a mission of his own. A group of Trackers followed him, for he had appeased their greed with a few coins and now they were his for the night. They hurried out listening to the Song of Evil so that their hearts also beat its chorus. They skirted the houses before turning to dart down the main street. Some saw them and scorned them and their evil, but these did not lift a finger to stop them, instead choosing to live worthless to their neighbors. So the doctor joined the shadows and became a shadow himself. They were at the prison door, listening to the conversation so sweetly ended. The doctor interrupted Kino's musings, hobbling quickly over from where he had been noting the preceding interaction.

His eyes had been blind to any change between Kino and Juana, and his ears deaf. Of course they had not spoken a word, nor grown mighty to behold, and so the beauty they had experienced had been withheld from the doctor's eyes, those eyes that devoured the poor townsmen. As he had watched them a plot grew in his mind until it overtook him and controlled his actions. Kino suddenly felt the presence of the evil, and looked up to see the doctor approaching, his belly jouncing with each step and his evil face marked across with lust for dreadful passions. Fear grew in the heart of the prisoner, so that it overtook him and dampened his joy and freedom. The doctor paused, wheezing a little from the effort. Then he beckoned Kino over, and Kino felt a power gripping him so that he felt he must approach the dingy corner of the prison the doctor had chosen.

The doctor was now very close, and his odor filled Kino with disgust. Kino renewed his old hatred for the man, and he scowled as he approached. Then the doctor bent over, exerting all the power he could over the poor man Kino. "Where did you hide the pearl?" he wheezed.

Kino winced and said he had thrown it into the sea and wished it would never be found again, and his defiance grew in his heart, for now he was glad that he had kept it from the doctor.

"I know," the doctor chuckled hideously, so that Kino quaked before him and seemed to shrink in size. "But I can take your Juana now that you are helpless."

"Juana." The word crushed Kino. He had forgotten her vulnerability. He looked at the doctor with anguished horror. In rage he pummeled his fists against the gate. The bars held Kino back, and only returned his blows by easily withstanding and leaving his hands bruised. Kino crumpled in defeat, and the doctor smiled, for he always relished the moments when he had at last hit his mark. He retreated now back into the darkness from which he came, slowly hobbling away in all his grossness so as to taunt Kino still further with the dreadful slowness of his saunter, a horror to behold, so that Kino hardened himself against everything about the man.

Within Kino grew a dreadful crisis as he considered the deed the doctor was about. Kino raged about the cell as one bereaved, ready to pour out on the world a cup of destruction for its wickedness. It only made him become very small and contained, unable to handle the wickedness. He loved Juana so much, and held her so dear to his heart. He had found at last a way where they could come together, and now it was to be torn away from him before the night had even passed. While he despaired over his loss, it brought him to think that if he had something to lose, then he was not entirely destroyed. If beauty still existed in the horror, then perhaps he could cling to that beauty, though the beauty of life and of even family might be torn from him.

Then the Song of Beauty took on another meaning for him, it was something more than just a song, but something of substance that could sustain him. Here he reached the climax of decision, for he saw on the one hand the great value of his Juana, and on the other the great value of the book. The price for both was high. Within him rose a struggle, for to accept one was to lose the other, and so he had to decide which was of greater value. In his mind he thought the book better, but his heart was drawn toward the woman so that he could not so easily decide. And then he decided. He decided that the Beauty was something much greater. And he said, "I want You," and so he let go of everything else to follow that of greatest value.

When he chose this, something snapped within him. Suddenly that small heart which had clung to something of the world let go to embrace something not of this world, something greater than this world such that it broke his small heart open to swell and expand. Now he sat stunned by the absolute wonder which he felt within him, and when he again considered his Juana, he saw that his love for her had indeed not diminished, but only changed. Kino saw her as valuable, for the Song of Beauty stretched around her so that though she was nothing compared to it, the music made her more beautiful. Hate had squeezed Kino's heart, compacting it so that he had a little heart unable to care for others. Now, however, the hate had snapped so that his heart grew to such a width with the love within him. Then and only then could he love the world around him. Now his heart was big, not because of noble compassion or love on his part, but because he had chosen to love something so big that it had stretched his heart. Before his love had been lesser than the object of love, and so to lose the object of his love meant he would lose his power to love, but now his love expanded around the little object of love so that his love would never be too weak.

Kino looked up then and saw the doctor. He looked different now, not so mighty and powerful. Kino saw a miserable old man, a man who hobbled around because of his excessive fat, a man who had to hide his face in the darkness of the night and who in that darkness walked alone. Kino was not miserable nor sick nor evil nor alone. And he looked on the man and had pity for him. It was an odd sort of feeling to Kino who had been taught to always control his emotions and to hate everything that hurt. Something was different now, so that as he saw the pain of this man, he had pity on him. Kino rose and the anger that burned in his heart was still there, but the love in his heart had made the anger different. He was mad at the wickedness of the man, and yet he felt sad for the actual man who had so little. Kino knew the doctor could not hurt him any longer, but that he could help the doctor. So he rose and gently called after him, "Come back."

Two words rose in the night and came floating along to the doctor. Never before had he heard such words spoken to him, for his venom had always killed. It made the doctor pause and turn and he looked back upon the man he had pursued as his victim, and he raged that this man could still stand after such defeat. The doctor did not want to turn back, but neither could he withstand the wonder of the beckoning. He turned around and approached Kino again.

A struggle raged also in Kino's heart, for it is not easy to forgive a man who has done such wrong. It had been easy enough to feel pity for the doctor when he had walked away, but now that the doctor was coming back it was much harder. Somewhere in his mind Kino knew that it was right to do this, and yet he hesitated. Despite his feelings he managed a few words, "You do not have to live this way." He did not have strength to add that there was a better way, but the words were enough.

Slowly the doctor understood something he had failed to understand before. Whether he believed it or not is another matter, for everyone makes his own decision, and whether he chooses what is good or wrong is not always clear. Indeed some even say they choose good and yet do evil, and some who are called evil do good. It is true that there is only right and wrong, but it is harder to say who will choose the right and who will choose the wrong.

The doctor had heard all that he needed to choose the good. He understood more than the words would appear to convey. He realized that it was not just this one action but the whole of his life that would be determined by his choice. In the past he had gained success by cheating and stealing, and yet he knew that still he sat alone in that great house. Here in Kino he had glimpsed what a new way might look like, he could see a new way to treat those who like Kino had come begging for help, and he wondered if indeed he could live this other way. Overwhelmed by his victim's words the doctor knelt and wept, and remembered all the misery he had brought to the world, and realized that the misery had crept into his own heart as he had brought misery to others and that his actions had made him a cruel man. The doctor wept, and his ugliness and wickedness was extreme to his own eyes, for the Song of Beauty had exposed his heart. Though there was a door open to him to change his ways, he had so accustomed himself to them that that he rocked and shook there, for it was hard to change and to admit his complete helplessness. Indeed, this is a hard thing. And so the doctor went out into the darkness choosing his journey, choosing as do all who are confronted with a choice. And choices are offered every day. Only a few have seen this power, and how it can change how one works and how one acts, and how one road is better.

CHAPTER 6

The Song of Evil is strong during the night, but during the day, the Song of Beauty becomes strong. Sometimes the Song of Evil persists into the day, and then the land is left in agony. At other times the Song of Beauty pervades the night, and what once appeared evil and dangerous appears fresh and wonderful. Just as the Song of Evil creeps and sneaks and invades, so does the Song of Beauty move, but it does not creep and sneak but flows and weaves and overflows. It rushes into old corridors and through shuttered windows like a pleasant breeze, and so covers houses with a scent of joy and happiness. It too sets out when its bearers bring it, and so this day it touched all those whom Juana touched and saw all those whom Kino saw.

Kino had awoken from the trials of the night to a new and fresh day, and he felt the Song of Beauty weaving through his body. Now the trial of his soul would be replaced with the trial of his action, for court would be held today. His spirit which controlled his action now coursed with a wonderful beauty which rose up within him so that he smiled. Before court, however, they would take him to the church to plead the priest for his atonement.

It did not take long for the town to awake and flow toward the church to witness the affairs of the day. The church stood in the center of a square formed by several of the nice cobbled roads that turned to dirt when they reached the places Kino lived. Cold marble structure and high arches formed its imposing shape, a shape which rose up in the midst of the poor shacks of the town. Though the townspeople of Kino's race often went hungry, the father always made sure to see the offering plate overflowing. Each of Kino's race would come and place a few meager coins in the coffer, either to find the priest peering in with shocked scorn or nodding approval. So was the manner in which the parishioners discovered whether or not they had received pardon for their many sins.

Presently the prison guards led Kino through the high doorway for the morning service. At the pulpit the father considered Kino's race with hard, unfeeling expression. Each of these entered humbly and quietly, with eyes fixed on the unadorned floor too scared to meet the father's eyes, and then each would kneel on the hard floor in the hard wooden pews. Of course those who belonged to the nice towns came in pompously, and acknowledged the priest unashamed and took places near the front, where they had payed their dues. Nothing stirred this pattern nor threatened the father's peering dominance on the proceedings. Nothing broke the coldness or lack of feeling.

As Kino entered the priest sneaked an interested glance his way before frowning in consternation to see his congregation turning its eyes to see who had entered. Each had turned at Kino's entrance, as if his presence of merely standing in the cold church had changed the atmosphere. Sternly, the father dropped his Bible on the pulpit, and the emphatic wrap of its sound brought all back to the ordered discipline. Yet all had felt it, the wave of power which had entered with Kino, and some hearts agreed with the priest and closed their feelings while others let the joy of the song fill their hearts. Though every response had been different, though some had quickly forgotten it, all had felt the stir of power coming from the prisoner. Then the guards prodded Kino in the back so that he continued to his own pew, and the service continued as usual.

When it came Kino's turn to approach the priest, he did so with humble power, yet the power was so great that it again startled the priest. Words fluttered up within the prisoner, so that he challenged the silence. As they poured out in a gentle flow, the power grew within him so that they came easily, though directed at the flabbergasted priest, "Would you continue to lead all your church in such human-willed discipline? Turn instead and accept the gift you wish." While the words came from Kino, the mass looked up to see how indeed it did appear that Kino almost rose from the ground, as if lifted by some awesome power. Indeed it was the power of the Song of Beauty, and his words came as softly and beautifully as the very song, for they came from a heart ruled by the song. Then it was quiet and so also the man was quiet.

Kino left the church without the atonement, yet he lived as guiltless it would appear as all those who had attempted to receive all the benefits of confession. Here was a great puzzlement to the people, and some approached Kino and asked him what was different. He responded in the same gentle and humble manner, and would explain to them with joy and smiles and then pass on as lightly as if he travelled effortlessly. So was the way in which the priest saw him go, and so was the way the people at the court saw him enter.

When he came before the judge, and all the witnesses accused him and the judge attempted to show an impression of disgust, Kino just listened calmly and was himself. Bitter accusers came and filled the court with their angry glares and sneers, so that at times the people would rise with them and offer shouts of disgust. And still Kino glowed with an inner happiness as he stood and accepted all the claims against him. He did not defend nor raise his voice to counter a mistaken account, but only waited in patience for the court to again settle itself down and reestablish justice. It vexed the people to see his patient humility, and so the accuser would come and rail against him with added fury, with shrieks and pointing fingers. And still Kino grew in patience and joy, so that the crowd began to note how he did not seem to even pay attention to the proceedings of the court, as if distracted by some dream or fancy.

The people grew more angry, and more accusers stood and complained. All had turned against Kino so that he stood alone, and yet did not stand alone, for he stood with a pillar of unalterable joy. Then the judge rose to make his decision, and the court grew silent except for the pleading words of the woman Juana. The time had come, and the decision was known to all. For a man can not continue to live in a town where all hate him. Instead the knife must find its mark, and the judge knew it would be better to kill him in daylight than to let the darkness cover up the deed.

And so the judge rose and began to utter his judicious pronouncements so that he would clear himself from all guilt, though the people listening had no idea of the meaning of the lofty words. When he reached the part just before the verdict, he paused, and the pause brought silence upon the whole room where the crowd prepared to cheer, and the pause was soft and gentle, yet sad and terrible so that an onlooker would have noticed the sustained sobs of Juana, and the caring affection with which Kino considered her. The pause fell upon the courtroom all intent upon whether the man should die or live, but then in the pause something else happened. Both of the doors swung open and the doctor entered. All heads turned, and in their thoughts came a pause from the concern of the proceedings to see this new curiosity, the doctor hobbling and tripping along toward the witness box.

Now all eyes fell upon the doctor, except those of Kino who continued to consider Juana with care. She too had looked up and restrained her sobs to see what sort of words the doctor might provide. The doctor cleared his throat in a strained huff which would have brought a laugh to all had he not been well respected in the town. Then he managed to squeak out a few words, of how "this man does not deserve to die," and "he has not done anyone wrong here," and "we should not blame him for our own poverty." That was all, and then he left. Soon a murmured hush spread through the chamber and grew louder. First they wondered what poverty the doctor could refer to when he lived in such a great house. But some understood the sadness of the doctor, and the poverty of his soul, and how when he walked, he walked alone.

What began as a mild murmur soon grew to a loud hum. Indeed it grew so loud in that rising humdrum of sleeping towns slowly awakening that the judge began to perspire in frustration and began to bang his gavel again and again. This only added to the noise so that it mixed in with the hum of discussion and made the judge only more and more frustrated, and the sweat began to drip down his intent face. Still Kino gazed upon Juana, and this time she returned his gaze and saw him standing in the midst of the hubbub unaware of the commotion. Eventually in the way of all people, the hum settled down so that when the judge finally realized that he need not continue tapping his gavel. He stopped then, so that all eyes turned to him to hear what he would say, and he began to say one thing and then another and flustered settled down again to silence. Several men came forward and explained how it would now seem more prudent to free Kino and allow him to live in the town, and a murmur of approval came from those gathered so that the speaker was encouraged to say further, "What seems to have happened is that there was certain information which we had not yet known of, so that in the end we will let you go." And though no new information had been offered, the crowd nodded with agreement for they would never have admitted their improper conduct.

So Kino was led down and some of the townsmen came and congratulated him and told him he should return and settle down again. They even offered to come over and help him with the new house, saying everything could be the same again, as if they thought they could with their words fill Kino. For they considered him a man of feeble heart, though it would have been obvious to anyone else how strong and well he looked. Then Kino said, "No. I must go." This caused a wave of disapproval to flow through the crowd, but Kino did not mind, and instead walked over to Juana and offered her his hand and said they would go. She rose then to stand alongside him, and as she did so a warmth entered her body sweet and strong as his gentle words.

Together they walked through the people who stood back in amazement to see them passing and once they reached the street they turned aside to head away from the village and back toward the mountains. Juana did not ask where they would go, not that she was scared, but that she did not care. For she stood by her husband, and now he was strong, and it was a strength she had never seen before. She looked at him, and the same strength began to feel her own body, and in soft admiration she said, "Now you are a man."

Kino turned toward her and looked with fondness upon her face, and saw how it had become gentle and kind, and told her, "And now you are a woman." Her soul leapt inside her, and it was not the words but the truth of the words which felt so good. And Kino also felt strong and absorbed the goodness of the sun and the warmth of the ground and wondered how he could have missed these blessings before. Then he forgot and did not care to think of why he had not noticed them, and instead soaked them in and enjoyed them, and though sometimes as he walked he would trip in a hole and though sometimes his legs would grow tired as he climbed a hill, he would continue to walk as a pillar of love because of his joy. It was not a dream he walked in, but the gladness of something as high as the clouds, and yet always higher.

Continuing, Juana began to understand that they were going along the same path they had travelled that day. Along the road they walked, slowly toward the remembrance of the past. There alongside the road grew the same trees, and here Kino almost stumbled in the same pothole, but it looked different in the day. It grew warm, so that sweat began to trickle down their tarnished faces. Travelers passed by. When the cart pulled by he saw the same poor couple and gave them a nod of recognition.

Kino and Juana saw the world differently. Now they were different, and the warm light which fell upon them warmed different souls and bodies. It felt good to walk on the sandy road, to enjoy the scampering of animals as they went off into the trees, and to accompany each other as man and woman. The Song of Beauty flooded their souls and bodies. It surged within them, and all around they saw the beauties around them. Even the long wheel ruts and sandy bumps took a fancy in their mind, so that at times one of them would smile and indicate an intricacy to the other.

They came gladly along, with the breeze playing with Juana's shawl, and the only sound the pattern of their footsteps, an occasional passer-by, and the flutter of the leaves on the trees. At last the sun began to set, and in their silent understanding Kino nodded to where they would stop, and Juana understood it would be the same deer clearing just a bit farther along the road. It came along suddenly, for Juana had grown distracted by the family walking toward them, and then the driver in the cart whom Kino waved at, and then the small herd of sheep several dogs kept along, and she had not noted her many steps. Then Kino drew her aside, and they entered the clearing.

As the light played in the leaves and darkness slowly fell, they opened the bag the doctor had given them. Inside they found a wonderful dinner, with rich cakes made with fruits, a pouch of water, and even nuts. They smiled then, and they would have smiled even more had they seen the doctor that night as he ate simple corncakes with a bit of a grin spreading his face. Then Juana went over to the trees and found one where she gathered a sweet liquid and brought it back in the pouch.

Then Kino sat with amusement to see a group of ants carrying there own dinner, and the lines of his face showed care. One ant fell into a hole, and struggled to get out. It would climb the wall and then its burden would become to great and it would fall. With the kindness of God, Kino reached down and lifted the ant and set it with its companions.

At last they spoke. Juana had watched him and a sparkle had grown in her eye. "I believe you will be a great man one day," she told him, but then added, "indeed you already are a great man." They laughed pleasantly, and among the trees in the deer clearing it was the most beautiful sound. And it made all the other sounds more pleasant.

"You too are a great woman, beautiful and wonderful," added Kino. "The town will love you."

"Will we return, then?" she asked, her eyes eager. And Kino nodded. "Will we have a beautiful life?"

Kino thought a little, and when he opened, Juana knew he had found the right words, "We will return and our lives will be beautiful. Sometimes mud will dirty our house, but this too will be part of the beauty." His words grew ever more wonderful and wise, so that Kino knew they came from the Song of Beauty. "Always our life will grow more beautiful, because we will be beautiful. Whether in loss or gain, we will always be happy." And Kino had never said so many words, so he paused, and asked her what she saw.

Juana considered, and noted how it was the first time he had asked her of her opinion. It felt good. Then her mind which had so long been contained opened up to new possibilities, for she had shut away her dreams long ago. "I see a snug house that does not leak the rain." It felt odd to say these things, but then she had so much more to say. She saw a family, and added, "We will live in that house, and we will love each other, and the children will run to see there father." She saw the family entering with smiles. "We will eat together with smiles and laughter. Then we will sit together outside our house, and children will come to play with our children, and men will come to talk with my wise Kino, and women will come and discuss how nicely the children play and how wonderful it is to see each other." She turned to see how Kino had taken it in.

He had watched her, and now he said, "I see the same thing." Joy rose up inside Juana, and she rested her head against Kino's shoulder, and as the sun disappeared they sat together, and when the moon rose still they sat together. And the night was beautiful, and the sounds of night delightfully mysterious, and the Song of Beauty was very strong.

In the morning they rose, and a husband's joy was in Kino's eyes, and a wife's softness was in Juana's. After breakfast they continued on the way. This was a marvelous adventure. In the desolate and waterless land before the great high desolate mountains scampered the two. Their hearts were light and joyful, and as all who have light and joyful hearts they rose to the high places, as if floating along. Two mountain goats could hardly have kept up with them as they bounded up the mountains and their feet squished the little tufts of grass. No longer did it seem a wilderness, for now a man and a woman inhabited the wilderness with a great expanding love.

And they soared. The way began to steepen, and still they leapt along to the high places. Soon they came to the little pool and the cleft in the granite where they had stayed and where their poor Coyotito had died. Kino looked out on the land and to his eyes it became a barren wasteland. The Song of Evil had attacked. He fell then to his knees with an agonizing yell, and his head fell against the rock floor of the cave and he moaned. Below Juana had stood and she too looked out and allowed despair to grow in her heart so that complete fear drove out her love for Kino and dreams for life. She too crumpled, and her body fell against the hard rock by the pond.

At length Kino rose and noticed his poor Juana. He cried out in a great peel like thunder and it snapped the spell of grief upon him. It was over. He leapt down the rocks and lifted Juana to himself. In his arms she slowly revived. When at last she opened her eyes, she looked up and saw his eyes sparkling down on her. And she knew that the evil was again repealed. They stood together looking down into the valley, and to their eyes it spread in a beautiful array, and they dreamed of how it might look better, and the music in their ears grew strong.

"Now we must go down from the mountain," said Kino.

CHAPTER 7

$\mathscr{E}$veryone in La Paz remembers the return of the family; there may be some old ones who saw it, but even those whose fathers and whose grandfathers never saw it know it well enough. It is an event that happened to everyone.

It was late in the golden afternoon when the first little boys ran hysterically in the town and spread the word that Kino and Juana were coming back. And everyone hurried to be with them. The sun was settling toward the western mountains and the shadows on the ground were long. And perhaps that was what left the deep impression on those who saw them.

The two came from the rutted country road into the city, and they were not walking in single file, Kino ahead and Juana behind, as usual, but together. The sun was behind them and it made their backs and heads glow golden, and they seemed to carry two towers of light with them. Kino had his arm around Juana, who was swinging the lunch bag gently at her side. And in it were fruits and nuts and berries. It had been stained but then washed, so that now its cleanness was a sweet freshness. Her face was full of vibrancy and with the easiness with which she shared her joy. She was as attentive and as close as if she brought Heaven. Kino's lips were rich and his smile spreading, and the people say that he carried love with him, that was as mighty as a father's embrace. The people say that the two were connected with human experience; that they had gone up to the mountain and then had come back down; that there was almost a magical involvement about them. And those who had rushed to see them crowded around them. They spoke with them and wanted to be with them.

Kino and Juana walked slowly through the city as though every part of it was important. Their eyes took in the right and left, the up and down as if now they saw it better. Their legs glided effortlessly, like willow trees in the wind, and they carried pillars of spreading warmth about them. And as they walked through the stone and plaster, city brokers considered them from unbarred windows; servants put there heads out and waved; mothers picked up their youngest children to look at them. Kino and Juana walked hand in hand through the stone and plaster city and down among the brush houses, and the neighbors came after them as if told, "follow me." Juan Tomás watched and saw Kino gesture and call out in greeting, and Juan Tomás responded fluidly.

In Kino's ears the Song of Beauty was as strong as the ocean current. He was concerned and caring, and his song had become a victory shout. They glided to the doorway of their poorly framed hut and then turned to see the people. And then they turned and looked down to the shore and saw Kino's broken canoe and still smiled.

And when Juana nudged Kino at the hut's door they looked and considered each other. And then Juana lay down the bag, and she dug among her clothes, and then she held the great pearl in her hand. They looked at its worn surface and it showed the marks of care. Wonderful power poured out from its simplicity. And it came out and quieted Kino's soul. And it came out and blanketed Juana with gentleness. And Kino heard the music of the book, wonderful and growing. Not just a dream but the real thing, as if the music had substance and you could hold it in your hand. Kino turned gleefully to Juana and held the book with her. She stood beside him, also enjoying the power growing inside them. She looked at the cover in their hands for a long moment and then she looked into Kino's eyes and said softly, "No, you."

And Kino drew away the book and brought it into the house with all his carefulness. Kino and Juana entered, winking and glimmering again in their home. Kino approached the little rug on the ground, and tenderly placed the book there at the center of his home, and they stood side by side watching the place for a long time.

And the pearl settled into the bosom of their family and its music spread throughout the house. The waving shadows danced on its surface in beautiful waves. It settled down to the core of Kino and Juana and rose up within them. And the pearl lay on the floor of their house.

And the music of the book rose to a rushing wave and took wings and spread.

It came to the boys of the town, to the boys in the town who had passed their days playing foolish games in the streets. And it was partially for this that they would have to start work very young, for their fathers would say it was not good for their children to play in the mud. It was not good for them to make balls of mud and throw them at each other and sometimes at the girls as well. A poor town does not have money to send their boys away to school. Besides, they do not want to send their boys away, as others do. But they can not make them behave, and so they only scold when they come home and try to bring some decency to the house.

This day, however, the boys left their mud statues and their teasing games. They left their houses where they bothered their mothers and the shops where they stole from the vendors. They left and came to the hut which had been burned and now was restored. And they asked Kino to tell them of his adventures and teach them of the book. So Kino had them sit down and told them stories late into the night, of the black pearl and the great pearl, of his son and of his wife, of great chases and terrible waves. And all the boys sat around with wide eyes to hear of such things, and then Kino would smile and they would smile, and he would become serious and so would they.

They talked late into the evening, and then at last Kino showed them the great pearl. The face on each boy glowed to see it, and they crowded around with such hunger to just consider its wonderful pages that Kino had to push them back and take them outside to teach them of it. And though they had loved every tale before, this book they loved even more, and they did not want Kino to stop. But at last as the last rays of light fled from the sky, Kino closed the book and told them to come back tomorrow. So the boys reluctantly trickled away as they had come, in little meandering groups. When their fathers came home that night the fathers wondered why the house was clean and why the boys were calm. And the boys would tell their fathers all about the great man Kino who they all loved and of the many great things he said. Then their fathers would pat their heads and put them to sleep, and the boys did not argue but drifted happily away as if in a dream.

And the next day when the mothers awoke to attend to their chores, some found to their wonder that their sons had already awoken and cooked breakfast, and explained that they must soon be off to Kino. And when their mothers gave them permission, they would trot off happily, and their mothers would shake their heads in wonder at their little boys who so quickly were becoming men.

That day Kino received the boys with smiles and pats on their backs. He said they would talk and read more, but first they had work to do. And the boys strutted around feeling important to think that they should have work to do, and after they had all become dirty from the work of fixing Kino's house, they all ran down to the ocean and cleaned off. Then they returned and sat on the ground in a circle around Kino. Juana stood in the door of her house and she thought well of her husband. Her mind drifted to the men out fishing, and then she remembered the canoe with the hole in it. And she was glad. Gladness is a virtue, love and gladness is a song, and Juana looked with love on Kino and considered with gladness the broken canoe. And she remembered Kino's words, "we must return," and knew that he had been right.

Each day the boys would come and work with Kino, so that soon they sat not on the ground but on stumps of trees, and then not on stumps but on chairs. And then not in the street but in a field, and then not in a field but in a thatched arena. The boys would go home, and now they would not play in the mud or bother the girls or distract their mothers. Instead they would come home smiling, and help other boys and be kind to the girls and come in wanting to help their mothers. Juana would watch them go and think how much they acted like Kino and still so much more like themselves, as if now a hundred little Kino's left the house with a hundred different ways of being Kino.

The music came to the girls of the town. No longer did the boys chase them in the streets, and it made them curious. Several followed the troupe of boys one day and peeked shyly from behind other huts. Juana stood in the doorway, and she saw the little girls and her heart leapt to see them shyly looking on. Then she called out to them, and they came trotting up to her, delighted to be noticed. Juana sat them down and began to teach them also, and their brown and black eyes grew big to hear of such great things. The next day they crowded around her with new friends and asked her eager questions. The girls laughed with Juana and learned with Juana and watched how Juana loved. And so the music came to them also and in a different way.

When they left Juana and returned to their homes, they walked happily, feeling very good to have heard such great things. They would say good-bye to their friends in the streets and come in to their mothers and give them a little kiss. Many other things they did also, for they were like Juana and did many nice things.

The music came to the men of the town. In the evenings Kino went out to the town square to sit and think and be a part of the town. Then a passing boy would point him out to his father, and the father who had noticed how his little boys and girls had changed would approach Kino and say in a gruff voice, "What do you know?"

And Kino, who had been deep in thought would look up a little surprised. When he saw the gruff father Kino became a little amused and then he would smile with a knowing smile and say, "Not much" and return to his thinking.

The man would get a little closer and bend toward Kino, but this time he would ask something different, "Tell me something."

Kino would again look up, and his mouth would curl in a merry smile, he would wink at the boy and then at last reply, "I'm thinking."

And when the man heard this he finally would change his attitude entirely and say in an eager manner, with all of the demands and prejudices left behind, "I want to understand."

Then Kino would at last respond, and he would talk with the man. And when he had shared many things with the man and the man had shared many things with him, then the man would rise and look at the sun and say, "Well, its getting late."

Kino also would rise in agreement, and they would go back to their homes. But that night Kino would eat in the man's house, and when Kino would leave, both would know many things in their heart, and they would want to learn many more so that on the following evening they would again talk in the town square. And the more full a man became, the more like Kino he became, and the more he would want to hear more words from the great pearl. So Kino would return and teach the men of the town, and when the sun went down they would return to their houses content and full, and the fading sun would warm their backs. And when they returned to their houses they would congratulate their children and complement their wives, and when they returned to their work they would do it joyfully and creatively, so that new things were made and the town grew.

The music came to the women of the town. When at last they finished the chores of the house they too would wonder what was changing their children. They would wander to Juana's hut, and ask her some little question as an excuse to come in and see what was happening. Then they would leave, and they would talk with other women about what they had seen. After several weeks, however, one woman dared to ask Juana another question, "How do you get all the girls to behave?"

Juana would look up from the floor where she was teaching the girls and say, "That is not the question."

Then the woman became a little vexed and almost left in a fuss, but instead turned and around, because still she was curious, "Explain to me."

And again Juana would only look up with a caring smile and say, "That is not the question."

This time the woman did not become angry but looked deep into Juana's eyes and said, "I want to understand."

Juana's eyes lit up and she told the woman to sit with them, and when they were finished she would talk with the woman. And when the last girl had left, Juana stood up and began to talk with the woman, and she spoke of her husband and the great pearl, and then the two would talk about boys and the girls, and when at last it came time for the woman to leave, the two would chuckle together and say, "Now we know a little."

Then the woman left, and her heart was glowing, and she knew that she would come back to learn more. And as the days passed by, other women came, and soon Juana would have to leave her girls in the afternoon to talk with the woman who came to her door to learn. And when the women left, they went away joyful, and they shared the treasures they had learned with their families. They would embrace their children and say encouraging words to their husbands, and they would make their rice cakes tastier, and the house neater, and the family lovelier. When the families would finish their meals, they would laugh together instead of scold, and still the children went to bed on time. Afterward the man and woman would talk together, and they would speak of the many good things they had learned that day, and the many good things they had done.

So a community developed in the town. The boys came to Kino in the mornings, and the girls came to Juana. And when the shadows became long upon the ground, Kino would leave his work with the boys and go sit with the men of the town. Juana would send the girls home and soon the women of the town would begin to come, and they would talk and spend time together. All this had once been customary in the town, but it had been forgotten.

Indeed everything in the town was now different. The music came to the doctor, who for the poor families would trade his work for rice cakes. He would go out and look in the huts for those he had turned away, and at night when he had seen a good many people, he would return to his house and sit contently, reliving the joys of the day. Of how he had entered the remote shack that hardly supported its roof, and of its owner, the old man who never rose from his bed. His old wife tended him night and day so that she could never leave to work enough to find vegetables or work to repair the house. And the doctor had come to this house too, and talked with the man and the woman. He had given the man a little medicine and then had eaten dinner, for the woman had been able to leave and buy some vegetables. Then they ate the weak stew together, and the doctor laughed and the man and woman smiled, and they had not smiled for many years. And when the doctor left they were still smiling, and the man was sitting up in bed, and the woman was telling of how nice the doctor had been. At home the doctor also smiled, for he heard the Song of Kindness.

Even the priest in the church changed, for the music came to him also when the people of his congregation entered and brought with them joy and love and peace. After the service, the priest began to speak with some of them, and as they spoke he learned many things about the life of the townspeople. And when the people came the next service, the church did not feel so rigid or stuffy, and behind they saw the priest smiling. When they left, their hearts were filled instead of empty, and they spoke of how different it had been that day.

When the judge left the church, he also felt different. That week as he heard the cases of the town, and there were not so many, he could not prevent his mind from drifting away to the music he had felt in the church. And during the next week he could not stop thinking of what it would mean to bring the music to the courtroom. And during the next week he decided.

This week as a small crowd gathered to hear the case of two men caught in a fight as they battled over chickens, the judge himself went over and opened the door. Each person he greeted with a beaming smile and a light tap on the shoulder, to which the people replied with a suspicious glance. When all had entered, the judge returned and gently began the meeting, and even when he banged his gavel down to establish order, it rang with a kind, resonating sound, instead of a harshness like before. He regarded the men with an uncommon firmness. And when at last the case was settled, and he had demanded retribution twice over for the one man, and three days of service for the other, he went over to the men. He, the great untouchable judge left his seat and came to the men. He whispered words of encouragement, and then he said he would help them. The two men hardly believed the judge or the words or the kindness, but when they returned it was true, for the judge came by and saw how life was going. And when he returned, he found the men chuckling together about the silly punishments they had not bothered to charge the other with.

Juana and Kino watched the changes of the town. And when at last the night would come and it would be just them alone in the house, they would dream together and tell stories of how the pearl had come, and of the adventures of the day, and how great it was to see the changes of the town. Then they would smile and fall asleep content.

Each day they became closer and their love grew for each other. One day a new sound was heard in the house. And peeking in one would have seen a little baby waving its little arms on the bed. And it was a healthy fat little baby, and his name was Benito. He brought more joy to the house, and often, at night, travelers would hear inside the house the family laughing together, and Benito's little giggles would join in with the rich sounds of his father's chuckling and his mother's laughing.

Benito grew strong, and his belly puffed out and his little arms grew larger. Kino and Benito did many things together, indeed Benito was most always at his father's side. And Kino taught Benito a great many things, all that Kino knew and had seen and had learned. Benito listened well and perhaps he taught Kino even more things, but when a few years had passed the people in the town already began to say how much he resembled the great man Kino and how one day he would grow up to be a great man as well. And there was rest and peace for Kino and his family.

And so the Song of Beauty became the melody of the town. The music dwelt in the city, and it grew in a rising symphony. The boys who played in the streets became wise boys, diligent and helpful. Their kindness touched their mothers hearts, and they cared for all the girls in the street whom they called sisters. And their sisters returned the kindness with their own gifts and kindnesses, and with smiles for their brothers. Teasing and joking had changed to love, and it was like one great wonderful family where all the brothers and sisters loved each other and did good things for each other. So the family grew to contain the fathers of the boys, who learned from Kino and then returned with gladness to instruct and teach their children. And their children would listen happily to hear marvelous stories from their fathers, until at last they would drift off to sleep. Then the mothers who had listened joyfully and had been able to finish all the chores would take their children to bed and kiss them on the cheek and say how wonderful they were. Perhaps this is a bit too far, and yet it has been seen before and is even now seen in some parts of the world, and so we must continue.

These families who had heard and received the music danced to its melody all day, so that they did many great and loving things. When they had left their tasks, they would go to their neighbors and teach them also, and to the old men whom they would help out of bed. Their wives would go to the old women of the town and bring presents, and when they would leave a house they would say a blessing over it and the old man and woman would be well. And their hearts would be full and rich, and this would make health flow through their bones.

The streets of the town changed. For the boys would clean up the trash and smooth the bumps of the dirt. They would take out the rocks, and clean the mud off from the houses, so that soon the streets began to look nice and clean. The boys would chase the filthy dogs off the roads, and clean them and teach them to behave in orderly ways. In the center of town they planted trees and in time the trees grew and offered shade and fruit, and their lives became wonderful.

Shops brought in more wares, and the wares were nice gifts for mothers and fathers and sons and daughters, and useful tools and important materials. Soon the shops became stores, and the stores great giant buildings that smelled fresh and clean and brought many marvelous objects. And in the stores the scales were fair, and the containers did not deceive, and the labels did not lie. And if something cost too much for a poor lady, the owner would give it away, and when something did not function properly, the owner would gracefully accept it. And when a buyer was not as content as possible, a smile would still spread his face.

New stores opened, and new businesses. For many years a kind man ran a shipping company, and it at first made only canoes for the fishermen and pearl divers, but then it made larger vessels. And these vessels sailed the seas and brought new riches to the town. When a ship would return laden with great riches, the people would not crowd around with stunned delight and eagerness to buy the things of the ship. Instead those who did not need anything new would stay at home and live contently and rejoice that others would be blessed, and those who could use a bit of leather or a load of wood would trade as gentlemen at fair prices.

All were blessed, and none needed to fight or deceive. When such a spiteful man came to buy, his words would fall dead, drowned by the surging music of the gentle words. With a bargain he might return home, but nothing would come of the bargain, for though he might find some success, he never found near as much as the others, and still for his efforts received not the regard of the town but its pity. Indeed wealth came easily to the town, and when they returned after a long day of work they did not collapse and say how tired they were but say how good it felt to work, and how strong in spirit and mind they had become. And so wealth came easily. And many wonders were built by the kind man and his shipping company, and many more wonders were seen in the town.

Abundance came to all, and it came easily and naturally, effortlessly. They did not strive or work for wealth. In their hearts they already were wealthy, for the Song of Beauty soared in their hearts and was more lovely than all the treasures they found. And because they were wealthy and content in their hearts, the outside changed as well.

For many years the women had complained of their soiled gardens and muddy walks. But when at last they heard the music, somehow their gardens automatically changed. Some indeed will doubt this, and many peoples could not believe it. And so they came to the city to see with their own eyes, and they saw that it was true. And this also is part of the mystery of the hidden treasure which here was not hidden.

And men came to live in this city, and when they came they were loved and greeted and asked how they could be helped. And they wondered how the men of the town could care so much for them and take so much time to lavish on them, and still create so many new wonders. Then the men would smile and say that that was the secret, to care for others and find joy in the gladness of others, and then all else would come as well. And men from all nations came to see this kingdom and talk with Kino. They would come from afar to speak with him, and leave full of his wise words. Many indeed will doubt this, but it is true that men from all the world came to share in the riches and accepted the wisdom.

The people of the town also went out in the vessels the kind man constructed. They went into many countries and many nations and with them they carried stories and sights and sounds of what a great kingdom looked like. But most of all they told of Kino and the Great Pearl he had found, and when they spoke of this their voice grew reverent and their hearts grew solemn so that those listening drew nearer.

Kino himself was often seen in one of the great ships, and it was with the kind man he would sit. The two of them would tell stories, but their stories were deeper and richer and more wonderful than the stories of the townspeople, and it was for this that all came to hear from Kino. The two would sit up late at night with the sun diving into the ocean or lighting up the clouds in many splendid colors. For Kino had at last returned to the sea. It was a wonderful night the first time he went down to the sea again.

The night was perfectly pleasant, and the birds floated along on the currents of the wind. Kino stepped along carefully, and his eyes looked intently all around him, as if he was remembering old places, old items. He knelt on occasion, and peered down at the sand, or a piece of wood, or some other object. But then he would rise again as if this was not it. And so he slowly made his way down the beach.

And when he heard the roaring of the waves he remembered the great storm, and he became so overcome with gratitude for its passing that tears came to his eyes. Then he listened again to the waves, and they became a lovely melody surging within him, and he knew that this is how they should be heard. Still his mind turned away from the waves to look for something else along the ground, as if one mystery yet remained.

Then he noticed how alone he was, for the happy cries of children had at last faded and it was him alone walking the beach. And he remembered how Juana had at last left him that day, and that he had been alone, so helplessly alone and haunted by the terrible things around him. But now he enjoyed the solitude. And yet he was not alone, for the music spread within him, and its wonder emanated from him, and it brought gladness to all his steps. This time his musings brought not tears but a surging in his heart, and as he moved along his body left the stiffness of grief and shifted smoothly as if dancing, dancing to some melody playing within the soul. A dark object caught Kino's eyes, and he fell to the ground and began digging, but presently his digging slowed and he rose again, and left the rock he had uncovered in the sand.

Again he continued on his way, and this time the beauty of the beach filled his soul. And it made him remember how he thought that one day all things were dark and dreary. Now everything was bright and wonderful, and it filled Kino's heart with gladness, so that this time he stretched to his full height and lifted his arms out toward the sea, and tilted his head back and breathed in the awesome wonder of the sparkling warmth. At length he continued on his way, and the joy and gladness continued with him.

And here at last as Kino continued he felt something under his feet and stopped and looked down. Then he dug and dug, until the sweat poured down his face in little currents and his muscles shook at each pull. As he dug the object entombed in the sand began to take shape. And there were long wooden beams with mosses hanging on them. Long and rotting. And when at last Kino uncovered enough for its shape to be known, it was part of a great ship, part of the hull. Then Kino sat and considered its arching beams and rotting wood as if he was pondering some mystery.

He kicked his feet in the sand, and it came down on something hard. At this his heart raced and he leapt forward. It was the treasure chest he had found, and some would recognize its simple form and shape. Kino knelt there in the sand and considered, and as he looked out, he saw out bobbing on the ocean a great ship, one of the kind man's fleet. Then he no longer wondered what made waves rise or fall, or what made ships sail to distant lands, or what made men do such great deeds. For now he knew. And as he bent and opened the chest, he considered the wonder of its coming to his world, and of the sailor who had once owned it and kept the pearl inside. Then suddenly it came to him, like a strong whisper in his ear, for he thought of it so quickly, and the thought was so real. It was as if he saw the sailor standing in the great ship, and suddenly in his vision the sailor became clear, and he was waving a sailor's cap off the bow of the ship. The ship was leaving a great dock, and a crowd of people were waving and cheering on the dock.

Somehow the people became more clear on the dock, and the sailor knew them, and Kino knew them too. First there was a wife, and her hair was flowing in the sea breeze, and it was the sailor's wife. And by her were two cheerful daughters, and by them three little boys proudly wearing their own sailor caps and saluting their father. Suddenly the view shifted, and there were others cheering on the sailor, a short humble pastor, and a wise lawyer, a kind doctor, and farmers and friends. Then the ship left, and the people slowly left. And it was as if Kino was sitting by the sailor, and he listened to his words, and the sailor was saying to himself, "this is what we bring, this is what we bring," over and over to himself. At first Kino could not understand, but then the meaning of the words filled out. And suddenly when the sailor said "this," the images on the dock were brought again to Kino's mind.

Then the sailor turned, and if Kino had really been there Kino would have been looking him straight in the face. "This is the dream," the sailor said as he lifted a book in his hands, and it was the great leather book. And then he lay it down softly again and said, "I will bring the dream, for I have not forgotten it." And if the sailor had still been alive now, he would have smiled at the town on the ocean far away, and the man Kino, and said, "this is the dream." Then the vision faded from before Kino, and he was weeping, weeping in the sand.

Presently the little speck in the sand rose, and the little speck was a great man. He raised himself up, and a deep joy was buried within him. Strength coursed through him, and if a wave had come tumbling down on him in that moment, it would seem that his glowing power would create a bubble around him so that the wave could not touch him. His toes spread over the sand; his legs were like great oaks, and his body was straight and strong. He stood with great power, and the Song of Evil cringed to see him so. The man spread back his head and laughed, and it was a great laugh, a mighty laugh, a wonderful laugh. It spread to those in the nearby huts, and when they caught it they too laughed, for it was such a laugh as makes the spine tickle in joy and comes down into you and makes you join in, too. It was a laugh greater than normal laughter, for it came from somewhere deeper, somewhere stronger. Its cords were richer, higher, more lovely, for it emanated from an abundant heart, a marvelous spirit.

Such power of joy thrilled through the man that when he looked at the few huts by the shore, and the houses in the streets, he directed his joy on them as if casting wonderful beams of delight. When the man ran, he ran with strength and power, as swift as the spreading of the wind, as light as its calming breeze. He was wild, untamed by the burdens of society or family or foe. And so he loved them all the more, and his joy and love wove a cord around them and kept them strong and in place. Again he raised his head and laughed, and the wonder of his power was so strong that perhaps it was good that he was alone. And this was the man Kino.

Something raged inside him, mightier than the waves of the sea and the currents of the ocean. It was the great pearl. It burned within him, though its burning never harmed or injured. For this was the glory of the great pearl, it gave a mighty joy more rapturous than all, a wild mirth which spread and sung, a glorious power which always increased in those it burned. It is always greater, always stronger. The power builds great people, and great nations, and great kingdoms. And yet even these are only a dim light of the great intensity of the light which is the pearl. Night falls on kingdoms, majesty is blinded, but the power of the pearl is a never-ending brightness, its glory a ceaseless glory. To find it is worth all a man's life, to seek more of it worth all a man's days.

In it all things are held together, and in it all things are built up, and in it all things are fully known. It is a mighty kingdom. It comes when it is looked for, moves when it is received. Few nations have loved it, and fewer have received its love. Old men, sitting at their beds, looking dull and tired. Young men, working in the fields, dirt covered and sweaty. Old women, tending to the house, growing sad and crippled. Young women, chasing after children, ordering right and mighty. Then the pearl comes, for it touches those, the lonely, it touches those, the mourning, it touches those, the miserable. Old men, standing up again, looking warm and vigorous. Young men, pausing in the fields, standing strong and powerful. Old women, fixing up the house, fixing glad and joyful. Young women, calling after children, calling full of vigor. Families fast and loving, towns strong and growing, people great and mighty. This the pearl makes.

And so it was in the town. New cords were fashioned, the cords of love and care, tenderness and mercy. It brought the families together, and the rings of houses, so that all people waved and called their greetings, pausing to encourage. Indeed many more things happened in this town than would be possible to describe, for the music of the pearl was its melody, and the power of its wonder an always mightier sound.

And the music rose and swelled, and it grew so that it touched all and in all it grew. And by its music the people lived, so that all they did was with the pearl. And by the music the people loved, so that all their neighbors felt its power. And by the music the people lived anew, so that they mended the old houses and the old problems and the old bitterness and built again. And the music was the Song of Beauty, and the music was a great fragrance, a wonderful feeling, a marvelous vision, a delicious taste, a splendid song. And by the music the people lived, and by the music the people loved, and by the music the people lived anew. And the glory of the pearl grew and grew and rose and rose so that it was sung on many shores, by many friends, and many sailors waved, and many travelers journeyed.

EPILOGUE:

In a distant land a boy calls to another, and they excitedly race up and over the hill and look out. They look out to sea, and the one called says, "what is it?" and the other says he does not know, but that it looks to like something special. "What will it bring?" the follower asks, and again he hears the answer, "I do not know."

The ship bobs in the water. In the ship there is a hold, and in the hold there are crates. Cobwebs and dust cover them. Enough light shines on the nicer crates, near the light streaming in from above, to read their labels. The reader must discern what these say. They are adorned with many wonderful patterns, and many not so wonderful patterns. In them is chronicled the history of the ages. Some crates are rather heavy, so that it would take a great effort to lift them up and remove them from the ship. Perhaps that is why the cobwebs now gather. The captain sometimes yells to his crew, "we are sinking, remove the crates!" Then the sailors rush down, and they heave and shove. Sometimes in times of great danger, they heave and shove with such force that they manage to bring one of the crates and throw it over the ship. And their short strivings cease, so that they grin and sit back down. Other times when the captain startles them, they rush down, and because they do not have time to move the heavy crates, they move the lighter crates, the ones that their fathers told them never to throw away. Whenever a storm comes, the captain yells desperately to his crew, and they scamper to return to their work, but when the tempest passes, each sailor returns to the pleasures he had worked on before. So time passes, and the ship sails on, and sometimes it rises on the water, and at other times it sinks.

Yet we will not talk long of the ship, for this story is not to chronicle the paths the ship has taken or the cargo it now holds. It is not to argue which crate must go and which must stay. That is for the sailors to decide. But once upon a time, the captain of the ship drew near to the coast and in the storm of all storms the ship broke upon the shore. Though the captain died, a certain man of that land found the wreck of the ship, and helped to build it again. We have perhaps lost this story somewhere, so that we do not know any more of the story than this.

In the back of the hold the crates are different. Some are smaller as if holding treasures beautiful, but small. Others are larger, adorned with great care. Here the cobwebs and dust are the thickest. The sailors never venture here. And here, in the darkest corner at the farthest end of the hold is a chest a little apart from the rest. It has been so long that the men have opened the chest, that they have forgotten what lays inside. One must go there, through the cobwebs and dust, to open the chest and see for oneself.

On this chest there is a label. It is etched in the softest of marks, so that some have faded away and been replaced with the dark wood. Hardly enough light shines upon the chest so as to make out the words. It is dark and cold, and we must not tarry too long in studying the marks. Someone must have visited the chest, for it bears an engraving, just legible. It says this: "he found one of great value, and after he had gone away, he sold everything he had and bought it." Will you?

Printed in the United States
By Bookmasters